For Finley and Charlie

On a magical, faraway island,
Where raging rivers flowed,
Giant, jagged mountains,
Loomed over fjords below.

Deep inside a forest,
From a hidden, mossy hole,
A kiwi bird called Manu,
Left for his morning stroll.

He waddled over sticks and ferns,
As fast as he could go,
And wondered who would be the star,
Of this year's talent show.

A chance for every animal,
To show what they could do,
Juggling, magic, comedy,
Dance and singing too.

As Manu reached the bottom,
Of the pathway down the cliff,
He heard a little whimper,
And a rather sorry sniff.

A tiny turtle sadly sat,
On a ledge above the sea,
So Manu tottered forwards,
What could the problem be?

"I can't jump! It's too far down!"
The trembling turtle cried,
"My friends are all rehearsing,
And I'm stuck here on the side."

"Try taking a deep breath,
And count from one to ten,
Maybe you could close your eyes,
Then try to jump again."

After Manu's calming words,
The turtle ceased his tears,
And diving down towards his friends,
He soon forgot his fears.

Manu trotted on his way,
Happy he could help,
But as he reached a nearby grove,
He heard a woeful yelp.

A fuzzy bat with pointed ears,
Hung from an ancient tree,
So Manu toddled forwards,
What could the problem be?

"I don't know how I got so lost,
I must get to the show,
Our act won't work without me,
But which way should I go?"

"Please don't panic little chum,
Soar back into the sky,
The show's just past that craggy ridge,
You don't have far to fly."

At that, the troubled bat took flight,
Gliding way up high,
But as Manu headed through the trees,
He heard a weary sigh.

Perched upon a twisted branch,
In her twiggy nest,
A little, feathered fantail,
Was feeling rather stressed.

Glumly gazing at her tail,
A sorry sight to see,
So Manu plodded forwards,
What could the problem be?

"Oh look at my grey feathers,
I'll never win first prize,
Against those dazzling parrots,
They're over twice my size."

"Fantail, you're so elegant,
Your talent will prevail,
I could pick some flowers,
To decorate your tail."

So Manu scurried busily,
To collect the brightest blooms,
And positioned them with care,
In the fantail's splendid plume.

"Thank you so much Manu,
Maybe now I stand a chance."
Then the fantail flapped off merrily,
Keen to do her dance.

So Manu sauntered on once more,
Whistling as he went,
But moments later he could hear,
Cries of discontent.

Which creature could be making,
That loud and mournful plea?
So Manu shuffled forwards,
What could the problem be?

A melancholy penguin,
Sitting in a huff,
"I'm trying to do the haka,
But I'm not fierce enough."

Manu paused a moment,
"Now let me have a think,
Stare directly in my eyes,
And try hard not to blink."

So the persevering penguin,
Did what Manu said,
And performed his gripping haka,
Glaring straight ahead.

"Wow! That was incredible,
You really made me quake,
It's amazing what a difference,
A little change can make."

Manu journeyed onwards,
As the show was starting soon,
The animals were gathering,
Beneath the silver moon.

The time had come, the stage was set,
The lights were shining bright,
The crowd all settled down to watch,
The first act of the night.

The turtles dived in gracefully,
Swimming in formation.

The bats caused much excitement,
With their flying demonstration.

The flowery fantails hopped and twirled,
A captivating dance.

The penguins stunned the audience,
With their fearsome haka stance.

Manu watched on from the side,
But felt a little blue,
He wished that he was on the stage,
And had something to do.

Despite his twinge of sadness,
He cheered and clapped his friends,
And hid his disappointment,
As the show came to an end.

"We're happy to reveal,
That this year's winner is,
Manu the Kiwi of Kindness,
There's no talent quite like his."

The crowd all turned to Manu,
Blushing and wide-eyed,
"There must be some mistake my friends!"
The dumbstruck kiwi cried.

"I can't dance a foxtrot,
Or jazz or tap or swing,
I don't know any magic tricks,
And certainly can't sing."

"Your kindness is like magic,
Look at the joy it brings,
Your sunshine dances through our lives,
And it's your heart that sings."

So take a leaf from Manu's book,
For being kind is free,
The measure of your talent,
Is how you choose to be.

Be someone's umbrella,
When the skies are grey,
A simple act of kindness,
Can go a long, long way.

CPSIA information can be obtained
at www.ICGtesting.com
Printed in the USA
LVHW070722060721
691898LV00001B/66